Level 2 is ideal for children who have received some reading instruction and can read short, simple sentences with help.

Special features:

Frequent repetition of main story words and phrases

Short, simple sentences

There was a time when Lion did not roar.

"This is MY waterhole," Crocodile snapped at the animals. "Snap!"

"Stop it, Crocodile!" said the animals. But Crocodile did not stop.

7

Large, clear type

The animals came to see Lion.

"Lion, you are our king," the animals said. "You must come and help get our waterhole back from Crocodile."

"Lion, please do something to help," said Flea.

Careful match between story and pictures

8

9

Tinga Tinga Tales is inspired by
traditional animal stories from Africa
and the Tingatinga artwork of Tanzania

Educational Consultant: Geraldine Taylor
Book Banding Consultant: Kate Ruttle

Series created by Claudia Lloyd.
Text adapted by Jillian Powell
Illustrations from the TV animation produced
by Tiger Aspect Productions Limited and
Homeboyz Entertainment Kenya.
Artwork supplied by Celestine Wamiru.

A catalogue record for this book is available from the British Library

Published by Ladybird Books Ltd
80 Strand, London, WC2R 0RL
A Penguin Company

001

This edition MMXIII

ISBN: 978-0-72327-334-9

Printed in China

Note to parents, carers and teachers

Read it yourself is a series of modern stories, favourite characters and traditional tales written in a simple way for children who are learning to read. The books can be read independently or as part of a guided reading session.

Each book is carefully structured to include many high-frequency words vital for first reading. The sentences on each page are supported closely by pictures to help with understanding, and to offer lively details to talk about.

The books are graded into four levels that progressively introduce wider vocabulary and longer stories as a reader's ability and confidence grows.

Ideas for use

- Begin by looking through the book and talking about the pictures. Has your child heard this story before?

- Help your child with any words he does not know, either by helping him to sound them out or supplying them yourself.

- Developing readers can be concentrating so hard on the words that they sometimes don't fully grasp the meaning of what they're reading. Answering the puzzle questions on pages 30 and 31 will help with understanding.

For more information and advice on Read it yourself and book banding, visit www.ladybird.com/readityourself

Book
Band
7

Why Lion Roars!

Based on a script by Edward Gakuya,
Bridget Hurst and Claudia Lloyd

There was a time when Lion did not roar.

"This is MY waterhole," Crocodile snapped at the animals. "Snap!"

"Stop it, Crocodile!" said the animals. But Crocodile did not stop.

The animals came to
see Lion.

"Lion, you are our king,"
the animals said. "You
must come and help get
our waterhole back
from Crocodile."

"Lion, please do something
to help," said Flea.

Lion went back to
the waterhole.

"Crocodile," said Lion.
"The animals would like
to share the waterhole."

But Crocodile just said,
"So? Make me share!"

"Now is the time to do something. You must roar," said Flea.

Lion went to roar... but no roar came.

"You see! This is MY waterhole," said Crocodile. "Snap!"

Lion ran far away
from the animals.

"I am not like a king,"
he said to Flea. "I have
no roar."

"You just have to find
your roar," said Flea.
"Come with me!"

Lion and Flea went far away, to the Great Cave of Tinga Tinga.

"Lion, you are king of Tinga Tinga. Tell that to the Great Cave," said Flea. "Find your roar."

Lion went into
the Great Cave.

"I am king of Tinga
Tinga," he said.
"Who are you?"

There came back a roar,
"I AM KING OF TINGA
TINGA. WHO ARE YOU?"

"Please stop it now," said Bat. "That is a scary echo."

"Was that me?" Lion said.

"That was an echo of your roar!" Bat said.

"I did it! I have got a roar," said Lion. "ROAR!"

Lion went back to
the waterhole.

"Crocodile, I am king!
I TELL you to share the
waterhole with all the
animals," Lion said.

"Make me!"
snapped Crocodile.

So Lion said, "I am king of Tinga Tinga. Who are you? ROAR!"

The roar was so scary that Crocodile ran away.

All the animals went into the waterhole.

"Lion is our king," the animals said.

That is how Lion
got a roar.

"ROAR!"

How much do you remember about Tinga Tinga Tales: Why Lion Roars? Answer these questions and find out!

- ## What won't Crocodile do?

- ## Why do the animals ask Lion to help?

- ## Where does Lion find his roar?

- ## Who helps Lion find his roar?

Look at the pictures, then match them to the story words

Lion

Crocodile

cave

Flea

Bat

Read it yourself with Ladybird

Tick the books you've read!

For beginner readers who can read short, simple sentences with help.

Level 2

 Beauty and the Beast
☐

 Chicken Licken
☐

 Little Red Riding Hood
☐

 Nature Trail
☐

 Sports Day
☐

 Pirate School
☐

 Rumpelstiltskin
☐

 Sleeping Beauty
☐

 The Gingerbread Man
☐

 Sly Fox and Red Hen
☐

 The Tale of Jemima Puddle-Duck
☐

 The Three Little Pigs
☐

 Why Lion Roarrrs!
☑

 The Big Race
☐

 Town Mouse and Country Mouse
☐

 Dragon
☐

For more confident readers who can read simple stories with help.

Level 3

 You won't like this present as much as I DO!
☐

 The Elves and the Shoemaker
☐

 Hansel and Gretel
☐

 Harry and the Bucketful of Dinosaurs
☐

 Jack and the Beanstalk
☐

 Furi on Music Island
☐

 Poppet Stows Away
☐

 Rapunzel
☐

 The Red Knight
☐

 Available on the App Store

The Read it yourself with Ladybird app is now available for iPad, iPhone and iPod touch

App also available on Android devices